DREAMWORKS

DRAGONS

How to Start a
DRAGON
ACADEMY

adapted by Erica David

Ready-to-Read

Simon Spotlight

New York   London   Toronto   Sydney   New Delhi

SIMON SPOTLIGHT
An imprint of Simon & Schuster Children's Publishing Division
1230 Avenue of the Americas, New York, New York 10020
This Simon Spotlight edition May 2017
DreamWorks Dragons: Riders of Berk © 2014 DreamWorks Animation L.L.C.

Vikings and dragons
used to be enemies.
Then Hiccup met his dragon, Toothless.

Now Vikings and dragons
live side by side on Berk.

Most Vikings are happy to share
their home with dragons.
But sometimes the dragons
get into trouble.

The dragons scare fish
out of the Vikings' nets.
They chase sheep out of their pens.
And they steal food.

Usually the Vikings
can forgive the dragons.
But some Vikings are angry
when the dragons eat their food.
They are trying to store food
for the winter freeze that is coming.

There is one Viking named Mildew
who is very upset.
The dragons ate his entire field of
cabbage!

"Stoick, you need to put those dragons in cages!" Mildew shouts. "If you don't, they will eat us out of house and home!"

"They don't mean any harm,"
Hiccup replies.
"They are just dragons being dragons."
Chief Stoick tells Mildew
he will handle the dragons.

That night Hiccup asks Stoick if he
can help with the dragons.
"You?" Stoick asks.
"If anyone can control them,
I can," Hiccup says.
Stoick decides to give Hiccup a chance.

The next day Hiccup and Toothless
go to the village square.
Hiccup feels confident that he can
get the dragons under control.

The dragons are up to
their usual tricks.
Hiccup watches as a Deadly Nadder
sneaks up to a house to
steal a loaf of bread.

Hiccup chases after the Nadder and places a hand on his nose. "No!" Hiccup says firmly.

The Deadly Nadder listens
and drops the bread.

But while Hiccup is training
one dragon, other dragons
make trouble all over the village.
Hiccup tries to stop them
but it is no use.
It begins to look like he is helping
the dragons break things!

Hiccup realizes he cannot train the dragons alone.

The next day Hiccup invites his
friends and their dragons to the arena.
"The dragons are out of control,"
he says. "We want them
to live in our world
without destroying it, but
they can't without our help."

Hiccup shows his friends
how to scratch under a dragon's
chin to get it to drop stolen food.

It seems like they are making progress.
But when they head into the village
to find dragons to train,
there are no dragons in sight.

Suddenly there is a loud noise!
Hiccup and his friends rush
toward the noise.
When they arrive, they are shocked.

The dragons broke into
the village storehouse.
They ate all the food
that the Vikings were storing
for the freeze!

Even Toothless is guilty.

Soon Mildew and the other Vikings
arrive.
They are very angry.
"You need to send these
dragons away!" Mildew shouts.

"You're right, Mildew,"
Chief Stoick says.
"We will cage them tonight, and
Hiccup will send them away
in the morning."

At dinner Hiccup and his friends
are very sad.
They don't want to send their
dragons away.
But Hiccup has an idea.

"The dragons are going to do
what they're going to do,"
Hiccup tells his friends.
"It's in their nature.
We just have to learn to use it."

The next day Hiccup and
his friends decide to work with
the dragons—not against them.

The dragons scare fish
into the Vikings' nets and
chase sheep into their pens.

The dragons plant food
instead of stealing it.
They even help Mildew
plant his field!

"Great job, dragons!"
the Vikings cheer.
Chief Stoick is so proud of Hiccup
and his friends, he gives them
their very own dragon training
academy.

Hiccup is excited.
He can't wait to begin.
"Dragons are powerful, amazing
creatures," he says.
"And I'm going to learn everything
about them."